JIMEEN

A great comic classic, now in English

'The intrepid hero of *Jimín Mháire Thaidhg*
now bursts upon an astonished world
in English translation.'
IRELAND OF THE WELCOMES

'Everyone deserves to read *Jimeen*
at least once.'
THE IRISH PRESS

'Irresistible'
IRISH POST

Pádraig Ó Siochfhradha was born in Dingle, County Kerry, in 1883 and died in Dublin in 1964. Under the pen-name An Seabhac (The Hawk) he published plays, new versions of old texts, and stories. *Jimín Mháire Thaidhg* was published in 1921. Since then Irish-speaking children have been able to enjoy his escapades. Now a whole new audience can share in the fun.

Jimeen

PÁDRAIG Ó SIOCHFHRADHA
(An Seabhac – The Hawk)

Translated by
Patricia Egan, Peter Fallon
and Íde ní Laoghaire

Illustrated by
Kieron Black

THE O'BRIEN PRESS
DUBLIN

This edition published 2000 by The O'Brien Press
20 Victoria Road, Dublin 6, Ireland.
Tel. +353 1 4923333; Fax. +353 1 4922777
E-mail books@obrien.ie
Website www.obrien.ie

First English language edition published 1984
First paperback edition 1987
First published in Irish in serial form in An Lochrann
First published in book form as Jimín Mháire Thaidhg
by Maunsel agus Roberts Teo., Dublin, 1921

ISBN: 0-86278-680-0

British Library Cataloguing-in-publication Data
A catalogue record for this title is available
from the British Library

3 4 5 6 7 8 9 10
00 01 02 03 04 05 06 07

The O'Brien Press receives
assistance from

The Arts Council
An Chomhairle Ealaíon

Layout and design: The O'Brien Press Ltd.
Illustrations: Kieron Black
Colour separations: C&A Print Services
Printing: Cox & Wyman Ltd.

 CONTENTS

1

My Mam

IT WAS THE MASTER who told me to write this. An account of myself. That's what he said he wanted. Who knows why he'd want such a thing!

Still, I might as well begin. I wonder where to start, exactly. The master told me to write my name at the beginning. But now it can't go first, because the top of this page is full.

I'll put it here: *Jimín Mháire Thaidhg* – Jimeen-Mary-Tim. I'm Jimeen. I have another name too: James Brassil. That's my Dad's name, but no one calls me anything but my mother's name. Mary-Tim is my mother, you know.

Mam is a wonderful person. We're all afraid of her. She's the boss in the house. You wouldn't be five minutes in our house before you'd know that every single thing begins and ends with Mam. That's why I'm called Jimeen-Mary-Tim.

I was born long, long ago. I can't remember when, but Old Brigid says it was thirteen years ago. She was the one who found me in the seaweed at high tide. They were all excited about me, and I just roared my head off.

All the women around used to come in to have a look at me.

'Hasn't he the great pair of lungs, God bless the child?' Peg-Nance used to say.

'Gracious me, aren't his two eyes exactly like Old Tim's?' Sheila-Owen used to remark.

'Don't be silly, for God's sake,' Mary-Andy used to say, 'are you blind? Don't you see that he's a Brassil through and through? Aren't those his father's two eyes and little snub nose?'

'I'd swear it's his mother he looks like,' Sheila used to say.

'Not at all,' Mary-Andy would answer, 'he's the spitting image of his father.'

The women were getting annoyed, until Big Betty spoke and solved the problem once and for all.

'Whoever he's like,' she said, 'he's a fine child, God bless him!'

I don't remember those things at all. Old Brigid told me them. It was she who took care of me when I was very small, I believe, because she discovered me that first day.

None of the little ones Old Brigid finds can talk or run or walk! I don't think I was ever like that. I have always had plenty of talk – much too much, Mam says. But I can't help it. There are things inside me that won't stay put. If I didn't let them out, they'd sicken me and I'd probably die.

I'm great at running, too. I caught the white calf yesterday. And I escaped from Mam when she made a dash after me for eating the cream cake. You see, that afternoon she was expecting Mary-Andy's daughter who was home from Dublin, and she made a cake for her and put a fistful of raisins and brown sugar in it. She left it cooling in the bottom of the dresser.

A fierce longing came over me when I got the wonderful smell, and when Mam went upstairs I stole the tiniest piece. I thought I'd die, it was so sweet! And then I went from bite to bite until I made a big hole in it. Boy, was I mad for that cake!

When I heard Mam coming down the stairs, I ran off and began to drive Little Donnagh's two calves out of the yard. I could hear Mam talking. She came to the door.

'Jimeen,' said she, and she didn't sound too fond of me.

'*Hoosh*,' I said to the calves.

'Jimeen I say,' she said again.

What would I do? I didn't know whether to go or stay. I couldn't make up my mind quick enough. That didn't do my mother, and she made a dash at me. I was keeping one eye on the door the whole time – I didn't trust her, you see, and I saw her coming. Away with me, and you wouldn't see my heels for dust. She followed me for a while but I was too fast. She had to give up.

I went in home through the window after that and I was in bed when Mam came looking for me again. I pretended to be asleep when she looked in. That didn't satisfy Mam.

'Have you said your prayers?' said she.

How well she knew that I'd forget them, with all the confusion. I had to get up again and go down on my knees.

Mam and myself didn't make it up for a whole week after the eating of the cake. There was no need for half the hullabaloo. Surely a poor young fellow, who is home all the time, deserves sweet cake just as much as Mary-Andy's daughter, home from Dublin.

2

Death to the Master

IF ONLY I WERE BIG! More than anything else in the world I'd like to be grown up – then everyone wouldn't be at me the way they are now. Boys have a very hard time of it. We can't do a single thing but someone gives out to us. The other day I hit Big Betty's gander on the side of the head with a stone, and Betty complained to my Mam.

When Betty went, Mam quizzed me about it. I did my best to explain that I wasn't aiming at the gander at all, but at Mickileen-Owen, and the gander just happened to get in the way. Mam grabbed me and gave me a beating for throwing stones, anyway. Did you ever hear the like of that? I tell you I paid for that gander.

At home they're after me until my heart is broken. I have to bring in the turf and the water; and I have to go to the outhouse for potatoes for the dinner. Then, if I'm out there playing a game of jackstones or throwing buttons, they're shouting and roaring at me that the cow has broken into the cabbage, and off I have to go again.

You know, I think they're not satisfied if that cow isn't straying into the cabbage patch – just to torment poor Jimeen. I can't imagine why boys are afflicted with mothers and fathers at all.

But when I'm grown up, not a cow or a calf will I herd. Nor will I help wind wool. Nor will I go to my aunt's house with the clucking hen. And I won't sit at the top of the table and do my lessons.

Nothing ever bothered me as much as those wretched lessons. There's no escaping them.

'Jimeen,' says Mam, every night, 'did you do your lessons yct?'

Once I chanced saying that the master hadn't given any. But she questioned Mickileen-Owen, and the good-for-nothing squealed on me. I didn't know a thing about it until Mam took the stick from the back loft and gave it to me across the shins. There was nothing I could do but escape through the side window. Off I went, looking for Mickileen-Owen, but he was afraid to face me. I asked him to come out so I could break his face, but he wouldn't. Then I began calling him 'pet' and 'eejit' and 'telltale', and he said back, 'Poor little boy, did your Mammy beat you? Oh! bold Mammy!' and he went on like that mocking me until I was in a right temper. I stayed a good while daring him to come out the door. But that was my mistake. His father was inside and when he heard me, out he came and warned me to be off.

Worse was to follow, because Mam was at the gable of the cow house and she heard him. She didn't rest until she had all the details of my doings. After he made his complaint, Owen went off, and when he was gone Mam started in on me. I wouldn't like to say what happened after that – I'd be ashamed. Mickileen-Owen told the other boys that Mam took down my britches – whoever told him – and that she beat me. I'm not saying she did. But I have to admit I wasn't able to sit down for three whole days – I was so sore in a certain spot.

Oh! indeed I'd rather be grown up, any day. But Mam's no worse than the master. He's always asking us to answer tricky questions – questions no one would bother with because they're not real at all. He's at his wits' end thinking up problems that will put us all in a fix: If a person had four pigs at a fair and got sixty-five pounds for them, how much each is that?

That's the kind of question the master gives us. Why should he, or anyone else, want to know how much each is that? If someone got sixty-five pounds for four pigs, shouldn't the master leave it at that and not be bothering us? But no, he won't; he's not that type.

One day he said to us – he was reading from a book: 'If a horse trotted ten miles in one hour, how far from home would he be in twenty-four hours?'

Well, I didn't know and I gave up. Some of the others did it. When the master came as far as me, he stopped.

'Is it that you don't know?'

'I don't, master,' said I.

Then he put the figures on the blackboard.

'Four times ten?' said he.

'That's forty,' said I.

'Twice ten?' said he.

'That's twenty.'

'And four?'

'That's twenty-four,' said I. He wrote down 240.

'Now, how many miles from home would he be?'

'Who knows?' said I.

'You and your wooden head,' said the master. 'Don't you understand that a horse travelling at ten miles an hour would do 240 miles in twenty-four hours?'

'He would not,' said I, 'he'd have to stop, or he'd fall with the hunger, or lose a shoe, or get a stone in his hoof or ...'

'Enough of that!' said the master, and he really had it in for me. 'Hold out your hand.'

He slapped me twice, two strokes of the stick that went right through me, and he put me down to the back of the school. I started crying.

I sat down there for a long time, vexed and full of spite. I was thinking about the kind of death I'd like to give the master. It would give me great pleasure to run up to him, punch him, a right and a left, and choke him, and dump his body in a bog-hole, with a big stone tied around his neck.

When I remembered the horse in his book that travelled 240 miles a day, I thought I'd tie the master to him and let him off without reins or harness, at 240 miles every five minutes, forever and ever, until he came to the edge of a cliff, where they'd fall down, down, down, and be smashed into smithereens on the stones – and no one would know which was which, a piece of the master or a piece of the horse. That gave me great satisfaction – to finish off the master like that.

After that I started writing questions that would put him in a fix! If there was a horse that could travel 240 miles in one day, how many miles could the same horse travel in 300 years. If Big Tim got fifty-nine pounds sixteen shillings and eleven pence three far-things for three sheep at the fair in Dingle, what would the master get for the horse that went 240 miles in twenty-four hours? How many ricks of turf would make a bag of soot? I was laughing away to myself, I was so pleased, and I never noticed a thing until the master was behind me. He let out a big guf-faw and took my piece of paper and read it out to the whole school!

They all roared laughing and I thought I'd go down through the floor with shame. Mick-ileen made a mocking face at me. I told him to wait until after school.

The master stuck my miserable page on the wall – for fun. I tell you, I was glad I hadn't written down the death I'd given him!

3

Mickileen Hits the Dust

AREN'T YOUNG GIRLS VERY STRANGE? All they're good for is screeching when you do something to them. There's a girl in our house: Cáit. She's my sister and younger than me. She's Mam's pet and Mam never beats her the way she beats me, and that's not right. I'm better than Cáit in every single way, but what good is that – I get nothing from Mam but the stick, and Cáit gets the pampering.

If Cáit does anything out of the way, all my mother gives her is a lash of the tongue. Even that makes the silly girl cry. If I was treated like that, wouldn't life be grand!

There's no good in Cáit. My mother tells me to play with her, and I do, sometimes. She's no good at jumping, or running. I played her for some nice buttons and won all the buttons she had in her box.

She started to cry and didn't want to give them to me, but I took them. She turned the whole house against me with her screeching; and when Mam came, she took every one of those buttons, and my own as well, that I had on a string.

She asked me where I got them all. I told her I won them from boys at school – and I did, too. But Mam wasn't satisfied until she looked at my britches. There wasn't a button left, but I'd made three holes and fastened the braces with two little wooden pegs and a three-inch nail! Then Mam played a dirty trick on me. She made me throw away the pieces of wood and the nail and hold up the britches with my hands. I spent three days like that until my heart was broken. But what really drove me mad was the way Mickileen-Owen mocked me. I couldn't run after him, you see, and he was tormenting me. On the third day I went to Mam.

'Mam,' I said, 'p-p-please put in the buttons for me. I'll never cut them off again.'

She looked at me. She was trying to make out what the hurry was.

'Ah, do, Mammy,' I said, 'and I'll be a good little boy.'

'Hm,' said she, 'what on earth's come over you? All the same, I'll put them in. But if you dare take a knife to them again, I'll skin you.'

And while she was sewing in the buttons, she was shaking me the way a dog shakes a rat.

'There, off with you now,' she said when she had them in and the braces were fixed.

I sauntered out the door and down the yard with my hands in my pockets pretending to hold my britches up. I hadn't gone far when Mickileen spotted me and over he came, with a mocking grin on his face.

'Hold-your-britches-up!' said he. 'Hold-your-britches-up! Ho! Ho!'

I wanted to draw him to me.

'Throw a stone now and see what happens,' I said.

'I will, Hold-your-britches-up,' said he, and bent down to get something to throw. It was then I leapt at him. When he saw me coming, with devil a hand in any pocket, he let out a roar and ran off screeching. I caught up with him and tripped him and stretched him on the ground. Then I sat down on him and pushed his nose into the mud.

'Now say Hold-your-britches-up, Mickileen,' I said and shoved a fistful of earth down his shirt. 'Hup, little horse,' I shouted, jumping up and down on his back. This gave me great satisfaction and I had plenty of sport for a while.

Just then Cáit came along and spoiled the
fun on me.

'Shame on you, Jimeen,' she said, and
looked at me with her two big eyes, about to
cry.

Believe it or not, I stopped. Somehow, all
the sport was gone.

'Shame on you, you big bully,' said she.

Didn't that make me feel ashamed! I've no idea why. I got up off Mickileen, not knowing what I was doing. When he got up, he was crying and covered in mud. Cáit went over and looked at him. Then she looked at me, her eyes filled with tears, and she cried. She tried to clean his jacket with a cockle-shell.

I don't know what came over me. I was ashamed. My self-respect was gone. I'd have given anything to undo all I'd done to Mickileen. At that moment, there was no one in the world I thought less of than Jimeen-Mary-Tim. Cáit was cleaning with the shell, with Mickileen holding the jacket for her, and the two of them crying.

I did it before I realised what was happening – I went over and took the shell from Cáit and started scraping.

'You're great, Jimeen,' said Cáit.

I couldn't say a word. There was something strange in my throat and eyes, and I was doing my best not to cry, but a big tear ran down my nose. I burst into tears. I didn't say a word but Cáit noticed and she ran over and put her hand on my shoulder.

'Good boy,' she said, and dried my eyes with her apron.

I was doing my best cleaning Mickileen, and nothing would stop me until the need to cry went away. It stopped at last when the mud was gone. Then Cáit laughed.

'Will you be friends now?' she said, the trickster.

I looked at Mickileen.

'I will,' I said.

'So will I,' said Mickileen.

'And you won't be fighting any more?' said Cáit.

'We won't, Cáit.'

'And you won't call each other nasty names?'

'We won't,' said the two of us, like eejits.

Then Cáit laughed and came between us, catching hold of our sleeves.

'Come on, we'll run,' said she.

Away with us both, dragging Cáit behind us, and all of us laughing. Mickileen's mother met us and looked at his clothes.

'What made you so dirty?' said she, looking at me suspiciously.

'It's how ... it's how I fell when I was ... racing with Jimeen, mother.'

She was still suspicious of me.

'And what knocked you down?' said she, looking through me.

I was sure there was another thrashing in store for me, but Mickileen saved me.

'And the place was full of mud; but look, Mam, Jimeen and Cáit helped clean me. I'm all right.'

And off went Mickileen, bringing the two of us with him.

Mickileen's a fine fellow. Now I know.

I'm still ashamed in front of Cáit. But I'm fond of her, and I won't ever make her cry again.

4

A Day at the Fair

I'VE A NEW PAIR OF BOOTS since the day of the fair. They're great boots, and I'm minding them carefully. They're sparkling clean up in the loft, and you'd see yourself in the shine on them. It was Mam who put them there, because I spent every minute polishing them and picking out with a stick the little bits of mud between the nails. And, yesterday, she made me take them off altogether, when it was raining.

You see, there was a pool of water in the yard, and I was standing in the middle of it, up to my ankles. I was trying out the boots, to see if they'd keep out the water. But Mam saw me through the window. I came out of that puddle fairly quickly, I tell you. I can't make any sense of Mam. What's the point of new boots that keep the water out if there's none around trying to get in? You wouldn't get any satisfaction out of boots if you weren't allowed to walk through water in them.

My mother didn't know why my stockings were all wet. She said there must be bad leather in those boots but she didn't see me yesterday morning trying to pull a sack out of Poulalin pond with a stick. We wanted to see how the cat was that we left there the day before. I reached out too far and my leg went from under me. Only for Mickileen-Owen catching me and pulling me back, I'd have fallen in with the cat!

When we brought in the cat, he was dead.

Mickileen said he'd come back to life again because that's the way with cats – they rise from the dead nine times. That's why we drowned him, you know, to see if this was true.

If he stays dead there'll be an uproar in our house, because he's our cat, and Mam's already asking about him. I've often gone down to see if there's any stir out of him but he's as stiff as a board. I prodded him and said, 'Puss, puss, puss', but he didn't budge.

Mickileen will have to put his own cat in the bag and drown him too in Poulalin.

Speaking of the fair, we'd a great day there. It had been long promised that I could go, and I was saving up my pennies. We got up – myself and Dad – at five o'clock and went to Dingle by moonlight. We had four beasts and they tried to go through every single gap we met on the side of the road and Dad was saying, every second minute, 'Jimeen, boy, run on and head them off', or, 'Hop in there, son, and drive out that one' when one of them strayed into a field. Often myself and the beast would make a dozen rounds of the field before it would enter her head to go back on the road again.

We met nothing on the way but when we came to the street and the fair-field there was more stock than I'd imagined in the whole of Ireland! Beasts and bullocks and cows and bulls and sheep, all of them bellowing and bleating and running all over the place.

There was a man making his way through the middle of the fair with twenty bullocks, and three men and their dogs behind them, with the men shouting 'How, how', and the dogs barking. They scattered everything in front of them.

There was an old man there with a cow on

a halter. A crowd of beasts ran in between himself and the cow and he had to let go of her. He was giving out furiously and complaining about people who have big herds of cattle and who drive the poor farmer off the better land. Our own four beasts were scattered three times; and I got the surprise of my life when Dad snarled at a tall thin fellow holding a stick and told him that he'd break his neck. I must say I didn't think my father was that rough.

The other man went off, and it's good for him that he did, because he was only a short distance up the fair when Dad went mad altogether.

At around eight o'clock the buyers arrived. They were all fat men with big coats, soles an inch thick on their heavy boots and leather leggings to the knees. They carried walking sticks and the signs of wealth were on them all.

They came towards us and each of them asked my father how much he'd take for the beasts. Not that they called them 'beasts', but 'wrecks' and 'skeletons' and 'half-dead things'.

'Eighteen pounds apiece,' said Dad.

Then they began to talk! At first, I thought that no more miserly and unreasonable man than my father had ever been born; and, as for the poor beasts, that anyone would be ashamed to admit they were his.

Sometimes Dad would get mad and he'd order them to the hottest and lowest seat in Hell. They'd reply that Dad would be there long before them, and tell him to take his four 'near corpses' home and give them a puff of smoke!

After a while, I thought the beasts might be worth something because one man offered thirteen pounds a piece and another

raised it to fourteen. They called Dad a 'stingy old rascal' when he wouldn't budge from the eighteen pounds.

Finally he took off ten shillings, and when the buyers went as far as fifteen pounds Dad came down another ten shillings. They were getting closer and closer until, in the end, there was nothing between them but half a sovereign. Then things got tough again. One of the men would come over and give a beast a slap.

'How much are these?' he'd say.

'Sixteen-pounds-ten apiece,' Dad would answer.

'Stretch out your hand,' the buyer would say, and he'd spit on his palm and slap it down on my father's.

'I'll give you sixteen pounds for them,' he'd say.

Dad wouldn't be satisfied and that buyer would go off in a huff, and I'd think he wouldn't ever come next or near my father again. But he would, again and again, and at last the bargain was struck and a big crowd gathered round ourselves and the buyer, and the difference was split, twice. Sixteen-pounds-seven-and-six we got.

When the beasts had been put on the train, we came out onto the street. Dad went off to look for the money and I went around inspecting everything. Dingle's a very big place, and there are a lot of people. It's mostly shops. As far as I could see, the people there are a thirsty lot because all the shops sell drink. I wonder what makes Dingle people so thirsty.

I met up with Dad after a while. He and two others were coming out of a house. I reminded him that I was there too and got a shilling from him. The others gave me a four-penny piece when they heard I was his son.

'He's a fine boy, God bless him,' said one of them.

'It won't be long till he's a great help to you, James,' said the other man to my father – but I took off, buying apples and sweets and biscuits. The shilling didn't last long at all. Everything's a fearful price, and you'd want a sackful of money to get any joy out of a day in Dingle.

Later, I went to find my father and found himself and Mam below in the middle of the street, looking for me. Mam was saying the poor little boy must be lost, or collapsed with the hunger. Dad was trying to convince her that I just wouldn't stay with him, and that I was in no danger.

Then they took me off to buy a pair of boots. Mam had brought a pair of socks from home. We were ages at it – I had to try on twenty pairs of boots before we were all happy. I think, myself, that no one was satisfied in the end but Mam. I wasn't too pleased with my boots because there were nails in them.

There was a lovely pair there in a box; the leather in them was soft and fine and they were as light as a feather. But the shopkeeper wanted thirty shillings for them and Mam said wouldn't I look nice walking through puddles and wading through pools in them. They got a fine strong pair for me for seventeen-and-six, and they were put on me. I marched out the door and up the street, knocking sparks out of the stones. The first person I met was Mickileen-Owen.

'Bad cess to you, Mickileen,' said I, 'get out of my way or I'll walk on you.'

Mickileen looked at the boots.

'They have you stuck to the ground,' said he.

I knew they were miserable boots. But I wouldn't give him the satisfaction of admitting it. Just then, as the two of us were walking down the street by the bank, didn't I put my foot on an orange-peel and slip and end up stretched full-length on the ground. It wasn't the boots that knocked me at all but that damned peel. But all the people looking on said I wasn't used to wearing boots, and even Mickileen was laughing.

I was going to try out the boots on him when I heard two brats from Dingle laughing at the clodhopper whose new boots tripped him up. I was raging and I gave one of them a sock in the jaw. The two of them attacked me, but Mickileen knocked one of them over, and the other fellow ran away. They spent the rest of the afternoon watching us, and calling us 'clodhoppers', among other things, but they wouldn't come within twenty yards of us because we were with Dad and Mam.

It was late when we got home that night. My father was in great form after the day and he kept saying 'It's a great life', and 'J-imeen's a good boy', and 'There's not a woman in Ireland better than Mam'. She kept telling him to shut up for fear anyone would hear!

I brought sweets and an apple for Cáit and we had a great time eating them as I told her all about the fair and about Dingle, and the lovely things there.

I've just been down to the cat, and I'm afraid
he's finished with this life. What will I do if
Mam ever gets wind of what happened?

5

Christmas

I MUST TELL YOU about the Christmas we had. Mam went to Dingle a few days before it – herself and Dad – and they took the horse and cart, with a creel and a box in the cart.

Mam had the money, and she took two geese – one for the vet and one for the bank manager, because he's the man who minds her money and she thinks the world of him.

While they were in Dingle, I went off to Glenadown with the big knife and some string and brought home a big holly bush, and I got some ivy in the ruins of the church.

As I was passing her door, Nell-Mary-Andy came out and was buttering me up trying to get me to give her some holly. She thought she'd make a right little eejit of me, praising me and calling me a 'good little boy', and promising me a Christmas present! I pretended, at first, that I wouldn't give her any. But, when I untied the bundle at home, I took a couple of branches over. I'm very close with Nell, you know.

Cáit was all excited when she saw the big load I was bringing in.

'Oh!' said she, 'we'll make the house lovely,' and she was looking at the red berries on the holly and dancing around the floor.

'Oh, aren't they beautiful?' said she. 'Did you ever see such a lovely red?'

That's the way Cáit always goes on, even if it's only a daisy or a bunch of cowslips. All the girls are like that, about all kinds of things.

I was hungry.

'Stop your messing,' said I, 'is there anything to eat?'

'Oh! I forgot,' said Cáit and she began to whisper. 'You won't tell what I've made, will you?'

'What?' said I. She laughed.

'I won't tell you, because you'd tell Mam.'

'I swear I won't,' said I.

'She'll kill me over the sugar,' said Cáit.

'What sugar?' said I.

'And because of the cream!' said she.

'Crikey, Cáit, have you made sweet cakes!'

'I won't tell you, I won't tell you,' said she, laughing and jumping up and down. Then she went to the dresser and took down two cups.

'Ah! Cáit,' said I, 'tell me what you made.'

'I won't, I won't,' said she, and she laughed, dancing and kicking up her heels.

She didn't see the ivy on the floor until it tripped her up and, lo and behold, didn't she break a big piece off the rim of one of the cups.

Cáit picked it up and she was trembling as she tried to fix it back in place. She started to cry, and then didn't she try to put the blame on me! I soon told her that it was herself and her jumping around. But there was no point in talking. All she'd do was cry.

I ended up feeling sorry for her.

'Give it to me, Cáit,' said I, 'and Mam won't ever know about it.'

I took the cup to the dresser and put it under two other cups with the broken side facing in.

'What will I do if Mam finds it?' said Cáit.

Then we each had a mug of tea. That was when Cáit brought out the things she'd made – little cream cakes with sugar icing on them. We got butter in the cupboard and I spotted a big pot of jam with the top tied tight. I cut the knot easily and we enjoyed all the things we had. We put a full spoon of jam on every bit of bread.

When we'd eaten our fill, the jam was well down the pot, but I tied the paper on again and put it back in the cupboard where it had been. It's a pity Mam doesn't go to Dingle every day!

Then I got a hammer and little nails and Cáit handed me the holly and ivy. We nailed it around the window, on top of the dresser, and over the fireplace. It was hard to fix it where there was no wood, and I had to drive big nails into the wall. From time to time huge chunks of mortar fell.

When we'd finished the house, we grabbed Sailor – that's the dog – and covered

him from head to tail with holly, and had a great laugh at him. When evening came we lit the lamp. The house looked lovely.

It was dark when Mam and Dad came home. We thought Mam'd be delighted but, to tell the truth, she caused ructions when she saw the lumps of mortar missing from the walls. I had to disappear until she calmed down. It's hard to please some people!

The following day Cáit told me what Mam brought from Dingle: nine big long candles standing in the creel, three of them red. They were as tall as the window, and she brought a box full of raisins, and one of sugar, and of tea, as well as a big barm brack from the shop. There were bottles too – some with yellow drink in them and others with something purple, and a big jug full of black stuff. She had a big lump of meat, too. I heard she brought apples, too, but I didn't even get one that night because of the damage we'd done with the nails. She put everything into the cupboard and locked it.

Next day Mam killed a goose and a duck. When the goose was cold, she put paper around its head and plucked it and left it hanging on the back of the door.

We had a great time on Christmas Eve. Cáit and myself got two big turnips and cut them in half and made a hole in each of them to stand the candles in. Then we stuck little branches of holly in them and Cáit put a frill of paper around them. They were lovely and we lit them long before it was dark; but Mam put them out again.

That night, Mam put potatoes and fish on the table for us but neither myself nor Cáit ate a single bit, because we knew other things were on the way. After a while, Mam took out the brack and cut it for us. Then she made tea, and gave us an apple each.

When Mickileen's father passed by the door, Mam called him in and gave him a drop from a bottle with three stars on it. She gave Dad a drop too. Then she got a drink for herself from another bottle and they all said, 'May we be alive this time next year', whatever they meant by that.

Big Betty and Mary-Andy came in next and Mam put a drop from the yellow bottle into two glasses, added sugar and boiling water, and stirred them with a spoon. At first I thought they wouldn't touch it.

'Oh! A drop of that would kill me!' said Mary-Andy. But she downed it all the same, and it didn't kill her either!

As the night wore on, a lot of young men came in and Mam gave them their drinks out of the big jug. When I saw them all drinking, I got an unmerciful longing for a drink, myself.

When Dad went out with Mickileen's father and Mam was talking to the women over by the fire, I took a swig out of the jug. It's a wonder the taste didn't kill me. I couldn't swallow it back, and was afraid to spit it out on the floor. I ran out the door with my mouth full. Mam saw me.

'Where are you off to, now, Jimeen?' said she, but I couldn't say a word. I opened the door and spat. She followed, and saw me coughing and wiping my mouth.

'Ha-ha,' said she, 'I wouldn't put it past you, you rascal. Weren't you the nosey one?'

It was horrible stuff.

It was late when we went to bed that night, because Mam was getting the goose ready for Christmas Day. She cleaned it out and washed it, then stuffed it with boiled potatoes and onions and salt and pepper and butter and loads of other things. She sewed it up with thread. Myself and Cáit were watching her.

On Christmas morning Cáit and Mam went to first Mass. Myself and Dad were left in charge. When Dad was milking the cows, I went to look at the things in the cupboard. I took an apple and filled my pockets with raisins. There was a piece of brack cut, so I took that too.

When I was closing the cupboard, a thought struck me – I took the yellow bottle and half-filled a cup. I tasted it, but boy, as bad as the black stuff was the night before, the yellow drink was seven times worse. It would burn the throat off you. I didn't know what to do with it. I called the dog and put the cup under his nose but he wouldn't look at it. All he did was sneeze.

Then I thought of another plan. I got a fistful of meal, wet it with the stuff from the bottle, and left it on a plate in the yard. The big gander gulped it all down. At first I didn't notice anything odd about him. Then he began to cackle. He stopped after a while, and started walking around with his head to one side. Round and round he went in a circle.

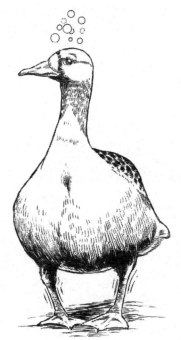

Then he stopped, spread his legs apart and started shaking himself backwards and forwards. He'd make the cats laugh. Then he lay down and closed his eyes, for all the world like Old Dermot when he dozes in the big chair by the fire.

Finally, he lay flat out on the ground, stretched his neck, spread his wings, and there wasn't a trace of life in him. It was as if he were dead. I was terrified that he'd die – and I didn't know what to do. I heard Dad coming in from the cowhouse and I ran inside. When Dad saw the gander he stopped and started talking to himself.

'Upon my word, but that fellow's really plastered,' he said. 'Jimeen,' he yelled.

I was sweeping the floor like mad. I came to the door.

'What did you do to the gander?' said Dad.

I stopped. I didn't like to hide the truth on Christmas morning, so I told Dad the story, in fits and starts. I could see he wasn't pleased.

'You'll pay for your tricks some day, my boy,' said he. 'And I suppose it was you finished off the cat, too, down in Poulalin?'

I thought I'd fall out of my standing. I didn't think a living soul knew about that. I felt sheepish then. I thought, of course, that Dad would tell Mam everything. I went to Mass and prayed all through it that God would keep me safe from all the trouble threatening me.

When I came home, Mam had the gander beside the fire, and he was recovering. She never found out what happened to him because, when Dad came home, she was trying to find out from him who'd come in that morning and got whiskey.

Dad was making a joke of the whole thing and wouldn't tell her. He threw me a look that left me feeling quite uneasy.

Still, Dad's all right.

6

The 'Wren'

WHEN I HAD FINISHED THE DINNER on Christmas Day I went looking for Mickileen-Owen. We spent a while skimming stones, then we smoked tobacco in a pipe that Mickileen had found lying idle in his father's pocket.

When all the tobacco was gone, we wondered what we'd do next. We were thinking of things for ages, but not one of them was to our liking. In the end we gave up completely. It was then the notion came into my mind.

'Do you know what, Mickileen?' said I.

'What?' said he.

'We'll have the Wren tomorrow,' said I.

'We will, surely,' said Mickileen, his two eyes jumping out of his head. 'And I'll be the Fool.' (That's the fellow who has the bladder, and hits everyone with it.)

'I'll be the Captain,' said I.

'And who'll be the Old Woman?' said Mickileen.

That was a hard one. We thought about Cáit and went to suggest it to her. She flew into a rage.

'You should be ashamed of yourselves, killing the poor little wren and going from house to house looking for money for it.'

'Wasn't it he who betrayed our Saviour?' said I, 'and doesn't he deserve to be killed?'

'Even so, the wren you'll have didn't betray Him,' said Cáit.

'Even if it didn't,' said I, 'its grandfather did, and they're all the same.'

There was no point in keeping on at Cáit. She told us to clear off with our old wren, girls would never do the horrible things boys do. She wouldn't go in any Wren.

Girls are useless.

Myself and Mickileen were in a right fix. Our Wren wouldn't be any good without an Old Woman. We tried all the local girls but not one of them would come with us.

'We might as well forget it,' said Mickileen.

'No, we won't,' said I, 'we'll put the Old Woman's costume on a boy.'

With that, we called the rest of the lads together and told them about our plans for the following day. They were all excited.

'Some of you will have to wear women's clothes,' said I. I didn't notice much excitement then.

'I wouldn't go in women's clothes,' said Tim-Larry.

'Anyone who won't do as I say can leave the Wren on the spot,' said I.

That made him listen.

'Where will we get the women's clothes?' said Smulc, 'and who'll wear them?'

'Tim-Larry and yourself, Smulc. You'll get them and put them on and you'll both be Old Women.'

'There's no woman in our house,' said Tim-Larry, 'except my mother and her clothes would be miles too big for me.'

That was a problem. I knew he thought he had beaten me. He got my hackles up.

'Don't mind that, Tim,' said I. 'It's no trouble. I'll get an Old Woman's costume for you, never fear. All be here tomorrow at eight o'clock, without fail. Now we'll go and catch a wren.'

We all got sticks and stones and we didn't leave a bush or a hedge or a lane unsearched in our hunt for a wren. But there wasn't a

trace of one anywhere. Smulc said it was likely they'd all gone home for Christmas, but I thought it more likely they knew that Wren Day was near and they all went into hiding for fear we'd kill them.

We had to go home without a wren. Mickileen wanted to abandon the plan again because we hadn't the little bird, but I said we'd pretend we had one in a nest in the middle of a holly bush, and we wouldn't let anyone look at it. Mickileen wasn't completely happy, but he gave in.

There was a hard hat and tail-coat in a big cupboard at home. They belonged to my grandfather before he died, a long time ago. I sneaked out to the stable with them.

I was looking for shoes too, but there wasn't a pair in the house that would fit me except a nice pair of soft boots belonging to Mam, kept on a shelf above the hob. I had my eye on them but I left them alone until morning in case Mam would notice. I made a mask from one of Cáit's bibs and took all the ribbons she had in a box, and put them on the hat. I found an old pike and tied a holly bush to the tip and put a nest made of moss in the middle of the bush. Since I was the Captain, I had to have a sword, of course. We'd never had a sword nor had any of the neighbours –

no one had ever needed one – and that meant I had to rely on a wooden sword I made from a board. I nailed a piece six inches long across it, where my hand would be.

When my own rig-out was ready I went looking for the Old Woman's clothes for Tim-Larry. There were none that would suit except Cáit's, and I was between two minds as to what I'd do. I searched Mam's room but there was nothing there that Tim could wear.

It was troubling me, going to bed. While we were saying the Rosary, Mam trounced me again because I said only seven of the ten Hail Marys. I don't know how many I said or didn't say, because, God forgive me, all I could think of was the costume for Tim-Larry.

Next morning I got up before the others. I put Mam's boots under my oxter. Then I went to Cáit's room and searched again for a costume for Tim. I was tempted in the end, and took a dress and some other things, and out through the window with me to the stable.

I put on my costume – the boots, the tail-coat and the hard hat with Cáit's ribbons streaming from it. Then I put on the mask and my belt and sword and I had the cut of a Wren Captain if anyone ever had.

Then I went looking for the rest of the gang. They were coming along one by one, and none of them recognised me until I took off the mask. We spent a good while dressing each other before we were ready. When Tim-Larry arrived I started to put Cáit's clothes on him. But there was a hitch – her clothes wouldn't fit him unless he took off his own, and that didn't suit him at all.

Only his shirt was left. But when the dress was on and the pointed paper cap on his head, he looked like a girl right enough. But the boots gave him away. They were his father's and too big for him. He dragged them along behind him with a flapping noise.

We had four musicians. I brought along a mouth-organ Cáit got from my aunt. I gave it to Tommy for the day. Mickileen had a tin trumpet which he gave to Smulc. Someone brought a big tin dish and was beating it with a stick. And another fellow had a bucket hanging from his neck – and the four of them were blowing and beating and hammering away, and they made fine music.

I gave the holly bush to Paddy-Dan to carry, and Mickileen-Owen was hitting everyone with a bladder we got from Young Tim when they killed the pig before Christmas. Some of them were wearing sacks, and others men's shirts and the odd one wore his mother's old skirt. Mickileen-Owen had Nell-Mary-Andy's blue blouse, and she didn't even recognise it until she thought about it the day after.

We tried Big Betty's house first. I had my sword drawn when we marched in the door. We struck up a tune and did a dance. We made a ring around Betty. She began to dance too, in the middle of the ring, and that was a sight. She was winded when she stopped and she had to sit down.

'God, you're powerful boys,' said she.

'Throw us a fistful of money,' said we, 'we'd prefer that to any old flattery.'

'Money, is it?' said she. 'Aren't you the rogues?'

And she was laughing as she went to the dresser. Betty's very plump and when she laughs, she shakes all over and you can't help laughing too.

She took down an old mug, found two bronze fourpenny pieces in it and gave them to us. We played again for her, did a bit of a dance, then off we went.

Next, we went to Mickileen-Owen's and got sixpence there. Then to Young Tim's. Young Tim was inside mocking us, saying we could neither play nor dance. But when we

were leaving he gave us a shilling, and his
sister-in-law gave us sixpence.

We'd great fun in Mary-Andy's house.
There's a stone floor there, you see, and we

made a great racket on it, dancing. When their big dog heard the music, he sat down on his hunkers, put his nose in the air, opened his mouth and started giving long mournful howls. You'd think all that ever belonged to him were dead. Nell was trying to work out who we were. Her mother suspected me from the start.

'God be with Old Tim,' said she, 'that's not how he'd like to see his beautiful coat end up.'

'Isn't it better than having it idle?' said I, playing the big fellow.

'Your mother will kill you,' said Mary-Andy.

That took the wind out of my sails. I had guessed there'd be trouble already. I wished I'd left my grandfather's clothes behind me. Mary-Andy noticed that her talk upset me.

'Look, Nell,' she said, 'you'll find sixpence in that purse. Give it to the boys.'

Nell went to the purse but she didn't give us sixpence, she gave us a shilling. Then she gave us each a hunk of bread with raisins in it. I like Nell.

We visited the other houses in the village one after the other and left ours until last. What Mary-Andy said about my grandfather's clothes and about my mother's anger –

that kept me away. Mam would definitely recognise the tail-coat and the hat, and that would be the end of the Captain.

What I did, eventually, was send the others to our house, while I stayed up the lane. There was a chance they'd get a shilling from Mam if she didn't see me with them. It's a good thing I stayed away. I saw them all go in the door, playing their instruments.

But, it wasn't long before the music suddenly stopped, and I saw them all jostling one another at the door, trying to get out. They stopped outside, looking at something going on inside, but nobody dared go near the door.

'Mam again, I'd say,' said I, and thanked God that I'd stayed out of her clutches.

It wasn't long before I saw the brave Tim-Larry coming out the door towards the others, and I nearly fell when I saw the cut of him. Not a stitch of clothes or of the Wren costume did he have on except what didn't belong to Cáit. It never struck me when I was sending the others to our house that Mam would recognise Cáit's dress.

Tim started whingeing, his hand over his eyes with the shame. I was sorry for him but, when I saw his face and the way he was dragging the big boots after him down the lane, I could only laugh. When Tim saw that he got mad.

'Stay away from me,' said he, 'you're the cause of it all,' and the crying and temper were choking him.

He grabbed a handful of stones in the lane and pelted them at me, crying and shouting at the same time.

We all burst out laughing.

'High jinks!' we said.

That was the last straw.

'Boo-hoo,' he sobbed and off he ran, across the fields.

In spite of all the fun, I was feeling uneasy. The thought of my mother's anger hung like a cloud over my head.

The Wren went off towards the forge and the houses over there, but the fun had gone out of it for me. When we went to Paddy-Tom's, he wouldn't give us anything. He called us an 'idle pack' and set the dog on us. The dog gave up when he got a blow of the bladder between the eyes. Paddy ran after us with his stick, but was wasting his time trying to catch us, especially since I had my mother's light shoes on.

We were tired of the Wren by this time and said we'd give it up. Anyway, we were getting hungry. We had twelve shillings and

sevenpence and divided it between ten of us
– one shilling and threepence each. We gave
the extra penny to Tim-Larry for the scold-
ing he got from Mam. Mickileen took it
home to him. Then they all went off, hurry-
ing with the hunger. But I was in no hurry to
reach home: I had doubts about the welcome
I'd get. I'd changed my mind about home. I
knew well that Mam was waiting for me and
that she'd want an answer about Cáit's dress
and my grandfather's coat and hard hat. I told
myself it would be best to keep out of her
way for a while, and maybe later on she'd be
friends with me again.

I went up to Mary-Andy's house. I
couldn't go to the stable for my own clothes
without Mam knowing. I was dead with the
hunger and hoped I'd get a piece of Christmas cake from Nell. I could have eaten a
huge piece just then.

Nell was inside with Mary-Andy and
Young Tim. When Tim saw the costume still
on me he started to jeer at me.

'He'll make a night out of the Wren yet,'
said he.

'Aren't you very fond of your grandfather's clothes?' said Mary-Andy, and she was
laughing.

Nell took hold of the hat and put it on her

head. It didn't look bad on her at all.

'Give me the coat,' said she, and she took it from me and began to put it on.

'Take off those things and don't make a show of yourself,' said Mary-Andy.

But Nell only laughed, and admired herself.

'Amn't I nice?' said she.

'Oh! lovely,' said Tim.

Mary didn't say a word.

'What did your Mam say when she saw you?' said Nell.

'She didn't see me yet,' said I, 'because I didn't go home.'

'Could it be you're afraid?' asked Nell.

'Well he might be,' said Young Tim, and told them what happened to Tim-Larry. Whatever about Cáit's dress, Mam went wild altogether when she discovered her father's coat and hat gone.

I knew well what was in store for me without Young Tim reminding me. Already I could feel my skin smarting and stinging from the beating I was sure to get.

'There's no need at all for her to be so hard on the boy,' said Nell.

Nell was great.

'And I suppose you haven't had any dinner?' she said.

I knew Nell was kind and that she'd keep on at me until I'd take something.

'Oh,' I said, 'I'm not hungry.'

I was, you know, but I was ashamed to admit it.

'Whether you are or not, maybe you'd eat a piece of Christmas cake.' I was in a spot. I couldn't say I would, and I didn't like to say I wouldn't. But Nell understood. She gave me a big chunk of barm brack and a mug of milk. While I was eating, I told myself that Nell was the most considerate person I'd ever met.

When I'd finished the meal, everything seemed much better and Mam was further from my mind, until I spotted the tail-coat. As it got late and time for me to be going home, I wasn't at all happy. The thought of Mam kept coming back to me. All I could think was that it would be as bad as the Day of Judgement as Big Betty often calls it – whatever that means. But I knew there was no getting out of it, and I got up to leave.

'Are you off home?' asked Nell.

'I am,' said I, half-heartedly.

'I'd rather go to the gallows,' said Young Tim.

They all laughed. I looked at Nell.

'Would you ever come with me and take the edge off her anger?' I said. I think Nell understood the state I was in. She got up.

'Indeed, I will,' said she.

My heart rose. Mary-Andy was laughing at the good of it. As we were going, Young Tim asked, 'Would it help if I went too?' And he looked at Nell.

Mary-Andy stopped laughing and she had a mischievous look as she searched in the corner for something or other. Meanwhile, Nell looked at Tim and called him to the door.

'Come on,' said I, and he came. It gave me

great courage to have the two of them with me, as I faced home. We went up the lane, with me in front and the others behind. They stayed at the stable door while I made for the loft to get my clothes and put them on. When I came back, we headed for the house. But I wasn't in front this time; I was dragging my feet.

'Don't be so scared,' said Nell. 'Come along.'

'Sure you won't let her kill me entirely, Nell,' said I.

'No, I won't,' said Nell. 'Buck up.'

I prayed to God and grabbed hold of Nell's dress and went in the door behind her. Mam was sitting at the top of the table and Dad was over by the fire. Cáit had gone to bed, I suppose. Mam looked at me. You'd hear a pin drop. My heart stopped and my legs began to tremble and I thought I'd fall over.

'You came,' said she.

I couldn't say a thing. Mam got up and took down the stick from the shelf above the fire, where she always kept it.

'Come over here to me,' said she.

God, I was cringing from sheer terror. I let go of Nell's dress to go towards the stick but Nell stepped in front of me.

'You won't lay a finger on the boy,' said she to Mam.

Good on you, Nell.

'I will too, and I'll skin him alive,' said Mam, 'because that's what he deserves.' She spat it out in rage.

'Ah wait, Mam, don't,' said Nell. 'The poor boy made a mistake, and he's sorry now.'

'He's sorry, I'm sure,' said Mam, 'hand him over and I'll show him ...'

'But he'll be a good boy from now on,' said Nell. Nell was doing her best.

'He will, when I've finished with him,' said Mam, and she made a dart around Nell to catch me. Nell jumped between us to protect me, but it's more than likely she'd have failed and I'd have been finished only that Young Tim came to the rescue. I'll never forget him for that. He grabbed Mam's hand and took the stick from her.

That was a great relief! Mam was furious, but they quietened her with sweet talk: wasn't I only a poor young fellow with no sense; you can't put an old head on young shoulders; sense never comes before age; wasn't it better to have me full of beans than a sickly thing hanging around the fire; sure I'd grow up to be a fine sensible man yet, with God's help; and a lot more of this kind of talk, until she calmed down. Tim changed the subject: bonhams eight weeks old were making five pounds in Dingle on the Saturday of Christmas week. And they coaxed Mam, like that, from her anger.

When they were talking, I stole off to bed, thankful that things were better now. I didn't get a wink of sleep, however, until I heard Nell and Tim going home, and my heart beat loudly until I heard Mam going into her own room. My Wren Day antics stayed longer in her memory than any other mischief I had got up to in ages. Every Sunday morning when she'd see Cáit's dress, with the black mark left on it since that misfortunate day, she'd bring it up again. If, by some chance, God would send a new dress in Cáit's direction, it'd be a great load off my mind.

7

Lost at Sea

MAM AND MYSELF haven't fallen out for ages, because I've been good. When I'd come home at night, I'd tell her I'd been up at Mary-Andy's house bringing in water and turf for Nell. Mam used to say I'd be as well off going and living with them altogether. I knew she was teasing me; but I'd tell her I wouldn't leave my own Mammy for anyone!

To tell the truth, I couldn't say whether I was mocking or not when I said that. Actually the way it is between myself and Mam is this: we're great with one another sometimes, but most of the time we're cautious of each other. The rest of the time is a battle and Jimeen is sad and miserable.

This is one of the miserable times. There's an out-and-out war between us. Maybe that's not the way to describe it because it's she who's fighting with me, and I've to pay for it. My heart is broken. She's been at me all week, and I can't please her.

I've brought in fourteen thousand buckets of water, and twenty million armfuls of turf, and I'm worn out from running, full gallop, doing messages for her.

What's the good of it all? After all my trouble, all I get is abuse. Once I was bringing in the turf and I brought a huge load thinking she'd be grateful; didn't a sod fall in the doorway and kill a little, new-born chick! Mam murdered me for that. I can't do anything right. Some misfortune strikes every single thing.

My mother made me help Cáit with her lessons.

'Eight by four?' said I.

'Forty-eight,' said the twit.

'You and your wooden head!' said I. That's what the master says to us at school – it's well for him he hasn't my mother in his class!

When Mam heard what I said to Cáit, she got mad at me. She grabbed me by the hair of the head and knocked some of the stuffing out of me.

'That'll teach you manners,' said Mam, and she shoved me off down to the room. Everything's against me and it's no good trying to make a good boy of myself. They won't let me be good. I don't think Mam would be happy unless she could be saying, all day long, how bad I am.

My heart was scalded when I was sent to the room. I had it in for everyone. I drew a picture on the floor of Tim-Nelly's old boat and danced and danced on top of it. I hated that boat because it was the cause of all my misfortune.

This is what happened. Myself and Mickileen-Owen had no football. The old one we had was in ribbons. You couldn't get a new one for less than ten shillings, and, after collecting eggs for a fortnight, we'd only four shillings and fourpence. I myself took the eggs from the hen that Big Betty had hatching for ten days. Mickileen got two shillings for them at the shop in Tobber. When four-and-fourpence was all we could

get, we had to come up with something else. We were plotting and planning for ages and the thing we settled on finally was to start selling lobsters. We fixed it for Sunday morning.

There was a lot of scheming between us. We agreed we'd take only four lobsters or, maybe, five. We wouldn't take more than five. We'd put them in a creel with seaweed around them and take them to Dingle, somehow or other. We'd have the football, coming home.

We wouldn't let anyone else put so much as the tip of a boot on that ball. Myself and Mickileen would be masters of it. I'd have it one night and Mickileen the next. Neither of us would be allowed to take the bladder out to blow it up.

On Saturday night we took the two oars from the side of Tim-Nelly's house and hid them in the bushes. The boat was afloat in the cove and we knew it'd be there in the morning. We both went to early Mass. When everyone was at second Mass we went as far as the Fort Field. We sneaked into the fort and let all the people pass. Then we took the oars and went on board the boat. It's a heavy old tub, and murder to row.

The wind was from the land and we moved east, close to the shore. We came to a float, took hold of it and began to pull it in, with our tongues hanging out, until a lobster-pot appeared at the side of the boat. There wasn't a thing in it. That wasn't too encouraging.

We came to another pot. There was a crab in that one with his claws apart trying to catch us. We let him go.

By then we were losing heart and Mickileen said we wouldn't catch a lobster at all. I told him to say a prayer and he was halfway through 'Our Father who art in heaven' when he remembered we were stealing lobsters. That put a stop to the prayers – he didn't like asking God to help him steal.

We came to the third pot and there was a monstrous lobster in it! When we put him in the bottom of the boat, he began to thump with his tail. We checked five more pots and got three lobsters. But by then we'd moved eastwards and were drifting out to Garranpoint.

I can't remember exactly what happened when we came to the Point. The sea was very rough just outside it and, when we got scared and turned to come back, the wind from the land and the tide took the boat and we were swept out into the open sea. As we were being carried off, the wind was getting stronger and we were growing more and more afraid. Mickileen started screeching and calling his mother, and then his face turned green, and he got seasick. I got frightened too. It occurred to me that God might be angry with us. With that, I threw the lobsters back into the sea to see would that take His anger away. Then I got desperate and beat the thwarts with my fists. And I hit Mickileen and told him to grab the oar. But we couldn't row because the sea was too rough, and the oars knocked us off the seat onto our backs.

I cried for a while, broken-hearted. I thought of Mam and Dad and Cáit, and called on Mam to come and save her little boy. And I said that she could beat me to her heart's content, and I'd be a good boy always, for ever and ever.

Mickileen stirred and told me to say a prayer and we went on our knees on each side of the seat, and said the Our Father and asked God and Mary and Patrick and all the saints to help us. We knew God wasn't too fond of us because of the robbing we'd done to buy the football. We promised faithfully we wouldn't steal a hatching egg as long as we lived.

We thought that might make things easier for us – there on our knees, gripping the seats, and the boat being tossed up and down, back and forth, by the raging of the restless sea.

I don't remember those things very clearly now. They remind me of the nightmare I had last year, when I thought Mickey-Thomas's bull was chasing me down the hill. Eventually, some kind of sleep or numbness came over me, and the next thing I remember is Young Tim shaking me, and when I woke I noticed there were five currachs around us and our boat was tied to one of them.

Mam was in that currach. My heart rose up when Tim put me into it and I saw her. I couldn't say anything; all I could do was cry. There wasn't a word out of Mam but she took me in her arms and held me close, and she put her cloak around me. I could feel she was all choked up, but it didn't make me at all afraid and I fell asleep and I didn't wake up until I was safe at home.

I was put into a big tub of hot water, and given hot drinks, and wrapped in flannels to make me sweat. I wasn't allowed to stir out of bed for two whole days. I was petted and pampered all the time.

When I got up and they saw I was in no danger, Jimeen got what was coming to him. Mam didn't beat me at all that time, but I'd much prefer the stick to the looks she gave me. She hasn't smiled at me for a week or called me a good boy. I suppose I am a bad sort and a rascal – that's what she called me the day I got up. But if I'm a rascal, it's not my fault. I try my best to be good, but I fail. I've done nothing wrong all week, and look! Mam won't smile or be friendly with me. What'll I do at all, if she stays that way? My heart'll be broken. She's too hard on me altogether. I know what I'll do. I'll leave her. I'll steal out the door and up the hill – up, up, up into the cliffs, and I'll go into a cave there, and I'll be sad and lonely, and Mam will come looking for me and she'll go away, sad and crying, looking for Jimeen, her good little boy.

And I'll be looking down every evening at the light in our windows and I'll know that Mam will be crying beside the fire, or standing at the door to see am I coming. But I'll stay in the cave on the hill, my heart full of sorrow, and death will be coming closer every day, and then I'll take this piece of chalk out of my pocket, and I'll write on the stone beside me:

'These are the bones of Jimeen who died in this place, his heart broken because his mam wouldn't speak to him.'

And years afterwards they'll find my bones and take them home to Mam. She'll be crying and wringing her hands, and she'll say, 'Oh, oh, oh, why didn't I speak to my own little Jimeen? Why did I break his heart? Ochone! Ochone!'

8

The Spy

SHH..., DON'T TELL A LIVING SOUL: I'm a soldier, and that's no lie. I'm in the Irish army and learning quickly to be a soldier – left, right, left, right, turning back, and knocking my heels together.

It was Young Tim who taught me the commands. Tim's the captain of the big boys here. It was he who made a soldier of me, and showed me all the right things to do. But I can't do them properly unless I have my boots on; bare feet make no sound.

One night Mam took the boots off me, when she caught me in the cowhouse with them on, marching around, turning and clicking my heels. I was stamping my feet on the ground, good and loud. Right turn, said I to myself the way I heard Young Tim tell the boys.

'Right, left, you little monkey,' said Mam, coming in the door and giving me two clouts, right and left! Then she caught me and shook me so hard my boots fell off. They weren't tied at all you see, and I'd no socks on. She said I was raising dust and it was going into the milk in the cooler.

Mam would hardly encourage you to be a soldier for Ireland. Even if I was kicking dust into the milk, wasn't that a little thing compared to the soldiering I was at?

And all the old women are like her, because when they're gathered around the fire, they're always giving out about people interfering with the government, 'who are so powerful, dear', and 'maybe 'tis how the pension would be stopped on themselves', and 'there's no chance at all that England will ever let go its hold on Ireland'. That's their kind of talk. But it's better to let them carry on; the poor things don't know any better. They're blind, God love them.

Since there was no one my age with me I asked Young Tim if Mickileen-Owen could be a soldier, too. He said yes, and the job he gave the pair of us was to be on the look-out and listening and to bring him information about anyone following the boys around there.

I reported all the old women to him, but all he did was laugh. Spies and enemy informers – these were what he wanted to hear about, he said.

From then on, Mickileen and myself never stopped looking for spies. We hid in the ditch, at night, listening to everyone who passed on the road. After all our trouble, however, there wasn't a spy to be found in the parish and we were very annoyed.

When the local people let us down we

thought we'd have some chance if we kept an eye on strangers coming and going. They were mostly beggars and tinkers. We spent many an hour watching them, and it broke our hearts that they were all decent people.

One day a man came from Dingle, with a donkey. He was limping badly. But, it wasn't Ireland or England that was troubling him. Another came and he was one-legged and had two crutches. Nothing would convince Mickileen he wasn't a spy disguised as a beggar and we watched to see if he'd put down his second leg, but he didn't.

Then a thin, red-haired tinker paid a visit to the place, with his wife and a clatter of children along with him. They tried every

"house during the day, and in the evening made for the crossroads, with their donkey and cart. They settled down there for the night. We knew they were hanging around and up to no good. The two of us planned to sneak out, when all at home were asleep, to keep an eye on the tinker and his wife.

I went out the window on a bit of a rope I had tied to the foot of the bed. I could have gone out the door without using rope, of course, but, there'd be nothing to that.

Mickileen met me in the yard, and the two of us went across the fields, towards the crossroads. The tinkers were still there and they'd a fire lighting and something roasting on it. I found out since that it was Big Betty's drake. When it was done, they ate it straight away, and gave the bones to the little children.

Then they all went to bed, except the father. He took the donkey and let him out in Paddy-Tom's meadow, and then, instead of going to sleep like the others, he set off for the houses again. That gave us a fright.

'Crikey, Mickileen,' said I, 'a spy!'

You could hear Mickileen's heart-beat and he was dumbfounded. We slipped off after the tinker. When he approached Mary-Andy's house, he crept along by the wall, stopping and listening every second. The moon was a tiny sliver that night.

'He's spying on Young Tim,' I whispered to Mickileen, when I saw the rogue go in among the buildings. My heart was in my mouth; I was sweating; my hands were shaking, and I didn't know what to do.

Mickileen was worse and his face was as white as a sheet. I saw the tinker again, crouched and creeping from house to house with something on his back. I told Mickileen to run off quietly and wake up some of Young Tim's comrades and bring them back to capture the spy.

He went off, and I crawled on my hands and knees behind the house, until I came to Tim's bedroom. I had a nail in my pocket and I started scratching on the windowpane – and it wasn't long until Tim came over. I warned him to keep quiet. He opened the window and I urged him to dress himself and hurry out.

'Follow me,' said I, 'I've found a spy.'

I crept off again to the corner of the house. There I stopped because I spotted my quarry again, sneaking between the buildings with his hat down over his eyes, eyeing the houses all the time. He'd something big on his back. He went quietly over to the dairy and took off the hasp, slipped in, and closed the door behind him. I bounded over and put the hasp back on the outside.

'Now, my boyo, take your ease there for yourself,' said I.

With that, Young Tim arrived and I saw Mickileen coming with four of the boys. None of them had his clothes on properly. I told them I'd a spy locked in the dairy, and how we'd spent the whole night on his trail. He'd have to be shot or hanged!

There wasn't a squeak from the villain I had locked up. I suppose he was on his guard, poor thing.

They all started questioning me and they were breathless with amazement. They spoke in whispers. Myself and Mickileen were trying to tell them the whole story, and we were breathless too. It took a long time to explain everything.

In the middle of all the talk, what did we see coming up the road towards us but a monstrous truck, with a big bright light on the front of it! We stood in astonishment looking at it and not a word out of us. It kept going until it came to the start of the village.

Then it stopped, and a crowd of men jumped out, soldiers and policemen. We saw them all coming towards Young Tim's house.

'Dammit,' said Young Tim, 'away with you, it's not safe here.'

We slipped away, without being seen, and when they stopped at the house, we stopped too and looked down at them. They searched the place, looking for Tim, but there was no Tim to be found. When he wasn't inside the house they began to search around the buildings.

When they went into Mary-Andy's dairy and discovered the tinker, there was great commotion and shouting, as well as strong talk from the tinker. They wouldn't believe that it wasn't Young Tim they'd got. They carried the tinker off, handcuffed.

When we came back down to the houses again, the whole town was awake and every family looking for its own. Mary-Andy kept fainting, and Nell was crying, and Tim was trying to calm them down. You can't reason with women. When Mary-Andy went to the dairy next morning, didn't she find the tinker's sack, with thirteen of her hens inside it, dead. When she told me, it all made sense. I was disgusted. After all the trouble, all I had caught was a robber – a robber of hens at that!

9

A Day on the Bog

THERE ARE BLISTERS on my hands, and I'm brown from the sun and the burnt skin is peeling from my nose like the skin of an overboiled potato. My bones are so sore I can hardly move.

All this happened when we were at the bog. If all of the others are as tired as me, I'm sure they won't thank the person who invented turf in the first place. The turf was for us, and I was kept home from school to drive the donkey to the bog with the food. For three days before the cutting, we were getting ready. Mam was baking bread and she kept four pounds of butter aside. She sent me to Big Betty's house for the large earthenware jar and to Mary-Andy's for the big tin jug. There was a grand sound from the tin jug when I struck it with a stick. With all the noise, I didn't hear Mam telling me to be quiet until she came up behind me and gave me a clout on the side of the head.

Next I was sent round the village looking for spades. Mickileen-Owen came with me and we didn't leave out a single house within a mile in our search for the spades for Mam.

This was after the business of the tin jug, you see, and I'd made up my mind to round up as many spades as I could to please her. We got nine altogether! It was all we could do to carry them home. Our tongues were hanging out with the effort and we'd let one fall every now and again.

But that was nothing compared to Mam's expression when she saw the load of spades coming up the yard towards her. I thought she'd bring the whole village down on me. She called me a complete eejit. That was my thanks after all my work. She never told me she only wanted two spades.

And about those spades, there's a fierce dispute going on. I couldn't remember where I'd got them, and when they were sent back, nobody got his own. What could I do about that? If anyone complained that he didn't get his own spade back – I was the one who had to pay.

Next morning, the first thing I heard was my mother calling us, loud and sharp. She said the whole morning was gone. I thought, from all her talk, it must be after ten o'clock at least. I rushed down to the kitchen but it was only half-past five! She sent Dad for the horse and me for the cows.

The kettle was boiled when we came back, and some of the neighbours were beginning to arrive. Young Tim came too. They all had pikes. My father tied the pikes and three spades across the back of the cart, and loaded a bundle of green grass from the meadow.

They all ate breakfast – there wasn't enough room for everyone around the table. Then the horse was hitched, and off they went, all jammed together in the cart, with the pikes and spades rattling.

When they were gone, Mam started fussing around. I had to get her a creel and some grass. She packed Big Betty's earthenware jar in grass in the creel. She loaded the kettle into a box, with Mary-Andy's noisy jug full of fresh milk, and the butter, knives, a couple of spoons, and eight tin mugs, a pound of tea, and a handful of sugar. She gave me eight ounces of tobacco too, for the men who were working at the turf. She put all the bread in a bag and threw it into the cart.

'Right, now,' she said, 'don't be so misfortunate as to lose anything on the way, and don't be all day on the road or the men will kill you. Up you get.'

I jumped in.

'Hup,' said I to the donkey. He gave a leap, and, out with the mugs onto the road. He covered a fair distance before I could stop him. That's a trick he has. He'd be making off while you're pulling at him, his neck bent in two and his head bent back as far as his tail from the pull of the reins, and all Ireland wouldn't stop him until he came to a ditch or something. It's no good saying 'Whoa' to him. Mam caught up on me with the mugs and said she knew well I'd lose them. That's what she says about everything – she knew it would happen. Mam's very smart.

Thanks be to God I reached the bog without further mishap. When I got there they were all giving out to me for taking so long. I wasn't long coming, but, to tell the truth, they were dying for the black stuff in the earthenware jar. No sooner had I arrived than they unloaded it from the creel and every man got a mugful of it – except Young Tim. He wouldn't drink it at all.

Tim was digging all day long and four men with pikes were behind him, throwing the sods from one to another. I was the cook. I gathered fir twigs and little dry sods, and I started a fire in the middle of the bog. I filled the kettle from a hole beside me, and it's a wonder the men didn't kill me because of that. I had to throw it out again and go off to a stream above us to get water. They told me to put the canteen of milk down in a bog-hole so that the milk wouldn't go sour in the heat.

I caught a newt under two sods of turf and a frog that was there also. I had the frog in my pocket, and when Big Tim was drinking a mug of the black stuff, I put the frog into it, without him knowing. I hoped he'd gulp it – because I'd like to see him with the animal

jumping around inside him. But when he went to drink, the frog appeared, and Tim let out a roar and threw the mug away from him. He immediately suspected Donnagh-Owen, and he began to get cross. There was a great argument for a while because Tim was raging and wouldn't listen to reason for a long time. I was on my guard! The frog jumped off the bank and disappeared down another hole.

After a while they set to work again, and there wasn't a word from anyone. But now and again, someone would break into a laugh and they'd be chuckling to themselves.

I had to go and work a pike. It was nice enough for a while but then the sods seemed to get heavier, and my palms got hot and the sport went out of it. I couldn't stop because the sods were coming, fast and furious; some of them would get tangled in the pike when I'd be throwing them and they'd nearly knock me over. They had me tormented and the palms of my hands were on fire, but there was no escape as those cursed sods were thrown around my legs. It was the mercy of God that made Young Tim remember the kettle.

'Jimeen,' said he, 'see is the water boiled.' That let me off the hook.

I went off and the first thing I did was

plunge my hands underwater in a bog-hole. That was great. Nothing ever made me feel as good.

The tea was made in the kettle. Tea and milk and sugar were all thrown in together and I never tasted the like of it. Thick slices of bread were cut and the butter spread in thick lumps on them and we sat on blocks of pine and turf-sods while we were eating. The men talked about turf-days and feats with the spade. They were talking about top-sods and lower-sods and the best of turf and wet clods. But I wasn't listening – I was trying to get a pull out of Young Tim's pipe without my father seeing!

We made tea again at about five in the afternoon and then they told me I'd done a day's work and I could go home. They were praising me too, saying I was great. I gathered my belongings after the tea, caught the donkey, and set out for home, singing. I brought a full creel of dry sticks for Mam and a lizard, wrapped in paper, for Cáit.

'Good boy,' said Mam, but when I offered the little lizard to Cáit, she shrieked! Girls are very peculiar. She said to take that creepy-crawly thing out of her sight.

It'll be a long time before I bring her anything again.

10

A Day at the Races

WHEN I'M BIG I'm going to have a currach and I'll take part in races and there won't be a single boat in any Kerry harbour that will come within an ass's roar of us. Everyone will be cheering and shouting 'Come on, Jimeen'. But there won't be a word out of me. I'll pretend I've done nothing great, though I'll be listening to them saying, 'Look, that's Jimeen-Mary-Tim – the man that won the race', pointing me out to one another. That's how it'll be when I'm big.

That's what I thought the day of the big race in Dillisk Harbour, a couple of weeks ago. It was a great day. I spent one shilling and fourpence on sweets and apples. Mickileen-Owen was with me and he spent a shilling. One-and-fourpence doesn't last long when you've to pay twopence for an apple that might be rotten at the core. And if you did spend a shilling on sweets, they'd hardly keep you chewing for half an hour.

The price of them would kill you.

I learned early how quickly the money would go, but I was scared to ask Mam for any more, because she'd know where I was going and I'd be grounded. Mam doesn't like currach races. When she wasn't looking, Dad slipped me a shilling.

It was a Sunday, and myself and Mick-ileen escaped from Mam and ambled off. We left our boots under a cock of hay in Mick-ileen's – because they were too heavy. At the top of the pass, we came across a donkey and the two of us got up on his back. That didn't speed things up, because neither God nor man could make him move. We had to leave him behind.

The whole world was watching the race – men, women and children. I never heard as much shouting, talk and argument. There were people selling apples, and sweets, and crubeens. The woman who sold dillisk was there as well, and there were singers, and a three-card-trick man taking shillings from people, right, left and centre. He'd give a crown to anyone who'd spot the ace of diamonds.

Once when he wasn't looking, Donnagh took the ace of diamonds and bent back the corner. Then Donnagh bet half-a-crown that he'd pick the ace. The man shuffled the cards and when Donnagh turned up the card with the turned-down corner, what did he have but the ten of clubs!

He was raging.

'You marked them, you crook,' said he.

The man took his crutch and hit Donnagh on the head. That was all I saw because others joined in. A great fight broke out and I had to leave.

I went down to where the currachs were.
That's where all the hubbub was, with everyone praising his own crew and knocking all
the others. When a currach took off across the
harbour, you'd hear someone say, 'Heavens
above, aren't they grand!'

Another man would answer, 'If there was
another currach alongside her, they wouldn't
look so good.'

'Yerra, nonsense, there isn't a crew in the
harbour today to touch them,' the first man
would say.

'The people from Coosportan! You're joking! What did they ever do?'

'They took the prize at Carrick Bay – and
they'll do it again today!'

'I'll bet you five pounds they won't.'

'You're on, and I'll raise you twenty
pounds,' said the other man, putting his hand
in his pocket. I wouldn't say he'd ever seen
twenty shillings!

The currach crews were changing; they
didn't leave on a cap or a coat or a vest. Everyone there was shouting at them, praising,
advising and spurring them on. You'd hear
a man yelling at one of the boats, 'Whatever
you do, Mike, don't let it go to Coosportan!'

It wasn't long before the two boats set off, the waves breaking before them, and the two crews rowing as if their lives depended on it, back and forth, back and forth, without stop or stay, the eight oars moving as one. The people on shore were going mad, running along the strand, shouting, waving their hands and their fists at the boats, giving them orders, and saying, 'Come on, you're great'. But the crews didn't hear them at all; they were rowing so hard you'd think their hearts would break.

Then Big Mike broke a rowlock.

'God almighty!' said everyone, thinking the race was lost.

But Mike found a new peg and started again with big, strong strokes.

'My! but he's a powerful man,' they all said.

Then the leader in the other currach broke an oar.

'Damn,' said the crowd, but they gave a mighty cheer when he hauled out a new one.

'What a man!'

That's how it was for all of two miles until they came to the second post where they had to turn back. Going around the pole, neither left room for the other, and the two boats got tangled in one another. The crews began to fight and I thought that someone would surely be drowned. But no, the other boats gathered round them and put a stop to the row.

But that was the end of the racing.

When Big Mike came back, he said it was the other crowd that committed the foul. The others said that Mike's crew crashed deliberately because they knew they were beaten. Each side believed its own crew and it wasn't long before the whole crowd was up in arms.

'Up Big Mike,' said somebody.

'Go 'way out of that,' said some clown. 'Up Coosportan.'

If there was quarrelling before the race began, it was nothing to the squabbling afterwards. Even the women were vexed and you'd think from their talk they'd been on the sea all their lives – every one of them found fault with the way the opposition rowed. You'd think women knew as much about rowing as Old Dermot who had spent sixty years in the bottom of a currach.

After we'd spent our last pennies on sweets for the road, myself and Mickileen went home.

11

A Night at Sea

I WAS DOWN IN COOS on Friday evening, watching the men putting the nets into the boats. There were fish in the harbour – harvest mackerel that had been in shoals on the surface for two whole days – and they were tempting the local people.

Old nets that had been years in the lofts or on the rafters were taken down, the holes were mended and they were got ready for the fishing. There are three currachs in our cove, and each one is owned by two or three people. Mickileen's father shared with Young Tim, and they took Donnagh-Peg with them as a third person.

It was a fine evening, and high tide, when we were loading the nets down at the landing place. I was holding the boat for Young Tim's crew, when they were sorting out the nets and tying stones for weights every couple of yards, and settling them in the bottom of the boat so there'd be no danger of the net getting tangled on the way down.

When the nets were on board Donnagh-Peg went home for his fishing-trousers and food for the night. Young Tim threw the sail into the bow and when he'd tied the boat to the iron ring, he and Mickileen's father also went home for clothes and food.

The sun had gone down and the sky in the west was the colour of copper. The sea looked as if it was asleep, its surface like glass. It was all so quiet it would make you sort of lonely, but it wasn't the kind of loneliness you'd try to avoid; in fact you'd stay there, and neither speak nor stir.

I didn't move for ages because I was trying to see Tír na nÓg way off in the distance. I couldn't. Young Tim told me that it's there, and that Oisín spent three hundred years in it without ageing a single day. Niamh of the Golden Hair told him never to return to Ireland. But some misfortune prompted him to come back to his people and, no sooner had he set foot on the soil of Ireland, than he became a withered old man, and he died shortly afterwards.

Wasn't Oisín the fool not to leave well enough alone? Too daring, I suppose.

When the fishermen were at home, I had a

great idea: I'd go fishing with them. All I had to do was climb in under the sail and stay quiet, and they wouldn't notice me until they were out too far to bring me back. It all came to me, like a shot. I went in under the sail.

There wasn't a squeak out of me as they were getting back into the boat. I could feel them putting out the oars and it wasn't long before I felt the boat moving. As it moved out of the cove I felt it rising and falling with the swell of the sea.

I was dying to come out and give them a fright but I was afraid if I did too soon they'd return and put me ashore. Every minute seemed like an hour. No one spoke for a long time but they pulled away, fine and easy. Then Mickileen's father saw something in the water.

'Is that a porpoise over there?' said he.

The rowing stopped. Young Tim spoke.

'There's a school of them there. They're going easy. That's a good sign. There'll be fish where they are!'

I'd have given the world to be able to see them, but I thought it better to keep my head down for another while.

They were talking then about the damage done to nets by those 'sea-pigs' and 'sea-sows' and the way the dogfish eat the fish out of the nets. Mickileen's father said they had three thousand horse-mackerel in the nets one morning and that the dogfish had taken a bite out of every single one of them.

I don't suppose they noticed they were talking about dogs and horses and pigs and other animals. Isn't it strange that all these animals are in the sea as well?

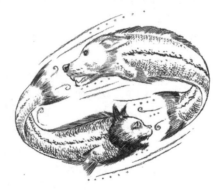

Eventually, I ran out of patience and put my head out. It was almost dark. The three of them had their backs to me and Donnagh-Peg was nearest. They were rowing away, and talking, and Donnagh was giving out about someone and the three of them were enjoying his story enormously.

I couldn't wait any longer. I got out quietly from under the sail and crawled over until I was just behind Donnagh. I grabbed him suddenly and said, 'Gur-r-r-r'.

Well, if you'd only one laugh in your life, you'd have to use it on Donnagh-Peg. He dropped the two oars and gave a roar.

'God almighty,' said he, and then he threw himself head first under Mickileen's father's seat. The others stopped rowing too and Mickileen's father blessed himself.

Young Tim stood up at the end of the boat and turned around to see what was all the commotion up front. When he saw me he burst out laughing.

'May I die of thirst,' said he, 'if it isn't Jimeen himself.'

Mickileen's father threw his hat on the bottom of the boat.

'Well, if that doesn't beat all,' said he.

We'd great sport then in the boat, out in the middle of the sea. Mind you, Donnagh-Peg was sour enough, and when they were wondering what to do with me, he said it would be a great relief to everyone if they tied a stone around my neck and threw me down to the bottom of a pool, because the Devil tempted me every single day of the year. Mickileen's father said that Aristotle himself couldn't cope with me!

They were a good while arguing and ended up deciding they'd keep me until morning, even though Donnagh-Peg kept saying that I should be brought home because if anything happened to me, my mother would blame him.

We started off again and reached the fishing ground in about half an hour. The two at the back stopped rowing and started letting out the nets; one of them looked after the floats and the other the weights. Donnagh-Peg was steadying the boat, and I was looking on.

I thought that once the nets were out, they'd be left that way till morning, while we waited above. But they were hauled up every hour, until five o'clock in the morning.

The sea at night is a wonderful thing. That night was pitch black and all you'd see of the land was huge dark rocks where you'd hear the waves breaking. When it's dark, there's a strange light on the water. I even thought the net was alight when they were pulling it in. 'Phosphorescence' Young Tim called the light. I had to touch it to see if it was hot, but it wasn't!

The first time we drew in the nets we'd only about fifty mackerel, so we moved off to a different spot and tried again. The second time there were only three and a dogfish. When it was inside the boat, you'd swear from the sound of it that it was a dog. Mickileen's father took out his knife and killed it.

We were drifting homewards all the time,

with no luck until four in the morning. And then they said they'd have one more try and, after that, give up. It was daylight already. There were a few fish at the top of the net and more and more later. As it was coming in, the men were picking out the fish, but when the second net came up we didn't bother with any picking – net and fish and all were thrown into the currach. In parts of the net there were mackerel in every single mesh.

There were so many fish the men had great trouble pulling up the nets, and the boat was listing to one side. We had our work cut out for us, but we managed finally to bring them all in. There was a heavy load in the boat, and the sides were only six inches above water.

There were fish and nets from bow to stern and up on the thwarts, and we were sitting on them. Young Tim said we probably had three thousand fish. Even Donnagh-Peg was satisfied, and he smiled – for the first time since the fright I gave him.

We headed for home, slowly, because of our load. It was a good thing the sea was so calm – if there'd been any swell we'd have drowned. But we moved along and, after a good while, we reached our own cove, below the houses.

Wait till I tell you what happened at home during the night. Cáit told me, the following evening, while Mam was milking the cows and I was locked in my own room. Cáit was talking through the keyhole. Apparently Mam was calling me to go for the cows and got no answer. She didn't take much notice of that – it happened often enough! She wasn't really alarmed until ten o'clock, when I should have been at home in bed.

When I didn't appear, she asked where I was, but Cáit and Dad hadn't a clue. She sent Dad down to Mary-Andy's house to see if I was there. When he came back without me the two of them went round to every house and when there was no news of me, her heart sank. Every boy in the place was hauled out of bed and questioned. Cowhouses, stables and haggards were searched, but there was neither sight nor sound of Jimeen. Dad rode to my aunt's house, five miles away, to see was there any chance that I'd gone there.

All the women gathered around Mam, telling her not to worry, nothing bad had happened to me and I'd be back the following day full of life. Mam was lonely one minute, angry the next. She was saying that her poor little foolish boy was surely finished this time, it was the end that had always been in store for him, because from the day he could walk he knew only misfortune and she anxiety.

Cáit said Mam was never so down-hearted. Mary-Andy and Mickileen's mother were encouraging her to look on the bright side and not be distressing herself over me.

'We were all young once with no sense,' said Mary-Andy. 'Let poor Jimeen enjoy himself while he can. Life will teach him soon enough that we were born for hardship.'

With that, Dad came back from my aunt's, and the horse in a lather. When they heard I wasn't there they lost heart altogether. The women couldn't say anything. They started whispering in groups, at the bottom of the house and in the neighbours'.

When daybreak came they left, in threes and fours, to search for me in the fields and ditches. And they went over to the cliffs, where they looked down, afraid they'd see poor Jimeen in smithereens on the stones below. They came to the top of the cove and looked into the water to see if my body was on the sand, covered in seaweed. It wasn't of course!

No one knew what to say. They were all quiet and, if they spoke at all, they spoke in a whisper. Mam came in and sat on the settle and no one could get a word out of her.

Things went on like this until half past five. Big Tim was on the ditch and noticed a boat making for the cove. He didn't show much interest until it turned around. Then he leapt up in the air and called the others.

'See that currach!' said he. 'There's an extra person on board.'

Because the boat was heading straight back to the cove, it was ages before they could confirm his story. When the boat turned again they could all see four people. Then their talk came back – everyone talking and no one listening, but everyone letting it be known that they knew well where I was. They just didn't like to say it!

Someone ran in to tell Mam. Out she came to the ditch and she didn't take her eyes off the currach until it entered the mouth of the cove. Then she went down to the landing place, her eyes ablaze. The whole village followed.

Before we came into the cove, Young Tim advised me to string a dozen good mackerel on a cord as a peace offering for Mam. I thought it good advice and had my fish all ready when we landed.

When we saw the whole village before us in the cove, we wondered what had brought them there. But when I saw Mam I knew well what brought her. I didn't like the look of her and the mackerel weren't much protection. I was cringing with fear, but I jumped out of the boat and went over to her. I was shaking as I held out the fish.

'I brought them for you, Mammy,' said I, but she didn't give me as much as a look – I might as well have been a crab. I thought I'd go down through the ground with shame, because the whole village was looking at me. Mam paid no heed and turned on the crew.

'God bless you all,' said she, 'you're kindly neighbours indeed. How well you made sure my mind was at ease through the night. I'm grateful to you, may you be spared any sickness all year long.'

She turned and went off.

They were so taken aback, they stood there, speechless. But I didn't want them blamed unfairly.

'You're wrong about them, Mammy,' said I, 'they didn't know I was ...'

'Listen,' said she, 'you go home.'

You can be sure I listened and I went on in front of her with my string of fish flapping against my legs, my heart in my mouth and tears blinding me.

I won't tell you the rest of that morning's story. I hate talking about it. But when the whole thing had blown over, my mind was made up. If I ever went fishing again I'd mention it to Mam beforehand. I paid for that bit of sense. But that's always the way with me. I never think first.

12

Mam's Plan

I COULDN'T MAKE OUT what was bothering Mam for the past fortnight. She'd be deep in thought, and sometimes she'd stop in the middle of her work and just stand there, thinking. Other times I'd see her talking to Dad, but all he'd say was, 'You're right. You know best, my dear.'

I did my best but I couldn't figure out what was on her mind. In the end, I discovered it by accident. Myself and Mickileen have a hideout in the cowhouse loft. I'm the leader of the gang. I was there one day, waiting for Mickileen, when Mam came in below and started talking to Dad while he was milking the cows. It wasn't long before I realised they were talking about me.

'It'll be ten years before he'll be a priest,' said Mam.

I nearly fell out of my standing when I heard that. Me – a priest! I almost gave myself away.

Then Dad spoke.

'Who'll do the ploughing and harrowing when I grow old?'

'Yerra, we'll manage. Won't we have Cáit, and a son-in-law to work the farm?'

They went on talking for a while and then they went away. I could hardly climb down the ladder with the fright. I went to bed, without pretending anything. When I saw Cáit next day, I said, 'I'm going to be a priest.'

She laughed.

'You will not,' said she, 'but I'll be a nun.'

'Ah stop,' said I, 'you'll stay here and Mam will find a big lump of a man to marry you and do the ploughing for Dad. You won't get out of it; Mam has it all arranged.'

The silly girl began to cry and who should hear it – Mam.

'Now what's wrong with you?'

'Boo-hoo,' said Cáit, 'I won't marry any good-for-nothing.'

Mam looked at her and then at me. I always thought a good run better than a bad stand, so I cleared off to Mary-Andy's house. Mary and Nell were inside.

'Well, what brought you over so early in the morning?' said Nell.

'Mam put the run on me,' said I, 'because I told Cáit they were going to make a match for her.'

'You little blackguard, what put that into your head?' Said Mary-Andy.

'I'm no blackguard,' I said, 'but Mam is going to make a priest of me and you'll all be calling me "Father James", and you won't call me a blackguard then.'

'Good God,' said Mary, 'you're joking.'

'It's no lie,' said I, and I told her everything. I couldn't help it, the damned thing wouldn't stay inside. That's my great failing, you see – my big mouth. I can keep nothing from anyone but Mam, and she finds out anyway.

No sooner had I made my mistake than the story got out all over the place. The night was still young when Mary-Andy called on Mam.

'Haven't you the good news?' said she.

'What?' said Mam.

'Little Jimeen going to be a priest, God bless him,' said Mary.

Mam got a great surprise. It left her speechless. She looked at me and I felt no bigger than a mouse, I was so scared. I saw she was annoyed that the news had spread already. I didn't like the look she gave me and went off to bed sheepishly. It was only half past seven!

I was sorry I'd said anything because I was sure I'd get a trouncing that night. But I didn't. When Mam was going to bed she came into my room with a candle and looked at me. I let on to be sound asleep, and wouldn't open an eye for a thousand pounds.

'Hm,' said she, and I knew she doubted that I was asleep. But she left, and I thanked God for saving me this time.

Mickileen and myself had a bit of a tussle the following day. When he saw me coming he said, 'Here comes Father James.'

I got into a rage and followed him up the field and gave him a bloody nose. Maybe that'll teach him manners.

But it didn't stop the rest of them, because they tormented me, calling me Father James, especially those giggling little girls. It was all my own fault, I shouldn't have opened my mouth to Mary-Andy.

For the next three weeks Mam was in a flap, getting things ready for me. She brought a new trunk from Dingle with loads of things in it – shirts and towels, and a comb for my hair, and a little bag to put my pyjamas in. There were pocket handkerchiefs too, and stockings, and the tailor made me two suits. I got two fine pairs of boots, and there wasn't a nail in them, but they squeaked when I walked.

I was going down the lane one day when Young Tim called me back.

'Tell me, Jimeen,' said he, 'what are those two boots saying to each other?'

'Ask your granny,' said I. I was raging with him, but he only laughed at me. He thinks he's real smart.

I'll be leaving tomorrow, and from all I hear, I won't have much time for writing this kind of thing from now on. I suppose there's hardship ahead for me. Mam says they'll put a spancel and bridle on me there, and I'll be crying yet for my mother and the fine life she gave me. If they're harder on me than Mam they must be terrible altogether. I don't feel good inside these days. I'm excited and anxious at the same time.

Mary-Andy came last night and gave me a couple of pairs of socks. Young Tim and Nell gave me a pound note. Mickileen-Owen came some time ago and he was half ashamed and said nothing for a while. Then he took a knife from his pocket and put it beside me on the table. There were tears in his eyes and he tried to say something, but couldn't. He ran out the door, crying. Cáit says Mickileen's very fond of me, and I gave her the pipe I'd hidden in the rick to give to him tomorrow.

My trunk is down in the kitchen, all packed. The last thing Mam put in was a big raisin cake. All the neighbours are there – because I'm leaving I suppose. Several of them gave me shillings and half-crowns and they were all advising and praising me.

Cáit has been crying all evening and there's not a word out of Dad. I'm not too happy myself either. Only Mam is all right. Nothing in the world would bother her.

They've all gone now and Mam's told me to go to bed. She followed me up to my room and spent a long time advising me. Then she hugged and kissed me and I saw tears in her eyes when she was leaving.

I can hardly see the paper I'm writing on with the fits of crying and loneliness. I'll have to stop, I suppose, and leave the pen aside. Anything I wrote about myself up to this is nothing but the whole truth. Now you know what I'm like. If I were like most of the others I know, I wouldn't have been so honest about my faults and you'd think I was good.

But it's hard for a boy to be good – it would

kill him in a week. I tried as hard as I could to behave myself at times, but I always break out again, in spite of myself. Everyone else is as bad as me. Nobody's perfect – except Mam.

I must go to sleep. God bless you. If you think I'm worth it, let each and every one of you say a prayer that God will direct *Jimín Mháire Thaidhg.*